Bark If You Love Perdy

by Jamie Simons
Illustrated by Yakovetic

Grolier Books

Published by Grolier Books

© 1997 Disney Enterprises, Inc. No portion of
this book may be reproduced without the written
consent of Disney Enterprises, Inc.

Based on the book by Dodie Smith, published by
Viking Press

Produced by Bumpy Slide Books

Printed in the United States of America

ISBN: 0-7172-8788-2

The rain was falling and the wind was howling all around the Dalmatian Plantation — but inside it was snug and toasty warm. And that's where 101 Dalmatians dozed and daydreamed as Roger, Anita, and Nanny planned what they hoped would be a very special birthday party.

"Nanny, do you think you could make enough dog food burgers to feed one hundred and one mouths?" asked Anita.

"And cake," said Roger. "There has to be plenty of cake."

"My pleasure," said Nanny. "After all, Perdita only has a birthday once a year, and heaven knows she's worth all the fuss."

Over in the corner, Pongo turned to Perdita, expecting to see a happy face. But instead she sat with her head on her paws, staring into the fire.

"What is it, Perdy?" Pongo asked gently. "I thought you'd be excited. After all, it is our first party since moving to the Plantation."

"I am excited, Pongo, especially for the children.

But I just keep thinking about our friends, the Colonel, Sergeant Tibs, Towser, and the others. I do wish there was a way they could be here."

"So do I," Pongo agreed. And then he resolved to find a way to make his beloved Perdita's birthday wish come true.

By bedtime Pongo already had a plan. As he gave the puppies their good-night lick, he whispered in their ears, "Meeting tomorrow morning after feeding time. Everybody gather at the back fence. Don't be late!"

The next day dawned bright and cheerful. Pongo let
Perdita sleep late — after all, he didn't want her to find out
about the meeting.

"Gather round!" barked Pongo as the puppies tumbled
into the backyard. "Here's the plan — so listen carefully!

I want you to go to Dalmatian Hill and send out the following message over the barking line: Long howl, yip, yip, short howl, two woofs, long howl. Which means: 'Tomorrow is our mother's birthday. Please send a birthday wish.' Remember, this is our secret. Now go!"

Off the puppies went, racing for Dalmatian Hill.
"Ready?" Patch commanded. "Begin!"
What a racket! Freckles was yipping when Lucky was yapping, and most of them just plain barked.
"Um, not quite," said Patch. "Let's try it again."

"Yip! Yap! Yap! Yip!" The puppies were all barking at different times.

"Oh, dear," said Patch. "We're just going to have to keep doing this until we get it right."

On a farm not too far away, Lucy the goose was flapping her wings with excitement. "What's all the fuss about?" she asked Towser the bloodhound.

Towser perked up his ears. "Let's see," he said. "It's the puppies. On the Dalmatian Plantation. Well, I'll be. It's been a long time since we've heard from them."

"But what are they saying? What? What?" honked Lucy.

"Wait . . . wait, it's coming in a little clearer now.

Something about Perdita," said Towser.

"What about Perdita?" asked Lucy.

"We're supposed to send her a fish," replied Towser.

"Send her a fish? What do you suppose that means?" asked Lucy.

"Beats me," said Towser. "Better call the Colonel."

Over on the Colonel's farm, a horse named Captain and a cat named Sergeant Tibs heard Towser's call.

Sergeant Tibs woke the Colonel, who listened intently. "Let me see. That's a woof. A howl. No, a bark. Towser is saying they need fish on the Dalmatian Plantation," said the Colonel. "How odd."

"All those mouths to feed, Colonel, sir," said Tibs.

"I'd better put it out over the line at once," said the Colonel. 'Perdita's puppies starving at the Dalmatian Plantation. Bring food. Quickly.'"

Back on Dalmatian Hill, the puppies were jumping up and down with excitement. "We did it!" woofed Lucky. "We sent our first message over the barking line."

"And a good one, too," said Freckles. "Send a birthday wish. Mother will love that."

"I don't know," said Patch. "Do you think our howls ran into our yips? I mean, will everyone understand?"

"Stop worrying! It was perfect, Patch! Perfect!" barked Penny.

Meanwhile, the all-dog alert was spreading from the country to the city. "Perdita's puppies weak from hunger out at the Dalmatian Plantation. Bring food immediately." "My heavens!" said the very fancy French poodle.

"I guess I could bring those little after-dinner treats my pet gives me."

When the Great Dane at Hampstead heard the news, he thought, "My biggest, juiciest bone should be enough to feed several puppies."

All night the word spread. "Trouble at the Plantation.
Need fish — or any food you can spare. Please help."

Throughout the city and the country, dogs saved part of
their dinner and their treats, tucking the tasty morsels into
whatever bags they could find.

At dawn a parade of dogs and other helpful friends —
big, little, long-haired, short-haired — were all making their
way to the Dalmatian Plantation with food to share.

Out at the Plantation, Anita, Roger, and Nanny were also up with the sun. "What a fine day for a party," said Nanny. "Oh, yes," said Anita. "Won't Perdita be pleased?"

"And surprised when she begins to receive all those lovely birthday messages from our friends," thought Pongo. "I know it's not the same as having them here today, but it's the next best thing."

By late morning, the party was in full swing. Perdita watched with delight as her pups raced from one game to the next.

At noon, Nanny began to ring a big bell. "Yoo-hoo, puppies. Pongo! Perdy! It's cake time! Come!"

"Let's do it properly, now," said Nanny. "Everyone, sit!"

"Now, now, puppies," Roger called. "Your mother gets the first piece."

"Oh, Roger," Anita said. "I know this is silly, but wouldn't it be nice if Perdita could make a wish when we cut the cake?"

But before Anita could blow out the candles on Perdita's cake, the air was filled with a sudden yipping, yapping, and woofing! And there, trotting up the lane, through the gate, and into the Dalmatian Plantation were dogs — lots and lots of dogs, as well as the odd horse, cat, and goose.

"Guests!" cried Nanny. "And look, they've brought their own food!"

"Well," Pongo said to their friends, "I asked for you to send a wish. But this is really too much. How can I ever thank you?"

"A wish?" said the Colonel. "I distinctly heard 'fish.'

Oh, my! We must have got it wrong."

   "Nonsense," replied Pongo, looking at Perdita's happy face. "You got it exactly right. You knew Perdita needed you and you came — and that's what friendship is all about."